AXED IN ALASKA

RAMBLING RV COZY MYSTERIES, BOOK 14

PATTI BENNING

SUMMER PRESCOTT BOOKS PUBLISHING

CHAPTER ONE

A cheerful whistle floated in from the balcony. Tulia Blake stepped out of her new apartment's kitchen and peered around the corner to check on her African Grey parrot, Cicero. Safely in the smaller of his two cages on her ocean-view balcony, he was preening his bright red tail while sitting on a perch in a patch of sunlight.

The view warmed her heart. Moving all the way from Michigan to Massachusetts had been no small task, and she had been a little worried that the thirty-one-year-old parrot might take some time to adjust, but he seemed right at home, and they had been moved in for less than a week.

It probably helped that he had accompanied her on a road trip around the United States the year before. Both of them were old hands at traveling now, but permanently moving to another state was something new for both of them. Tulia was more excited than nervous, which was good, but that didn't mean the nerves weren't there.

She hadn't moved to the little town of Loon Bay *just* for a man, but her boyfriend, Samuel Noble, was the major reason she had chosen this particular town to call her new home. It was a big leap to take for someone she had only known for a year, but they had been through a lot together, and unless they wanted to be in a permanent long-distance relationship, something had needed to change.

Since Samuel owned and worked at his own private investigating business with his partner, Marc, and she was a somewhat less tied down lottery winner, it had seemed obvious that she was the one who would make the move. It helped that she had also been itching to experience life outside of Michigan. She loved her home state, but her road trip had awakened a hunger for *more* in her that she hadn't been aware of before. Picking up and moving to a new state was just the sort of adventure she had come to crave.

"Breakfast is coming up in about two minutes,

buddy," she told the bird before she popped back into the kitchen.

Some people might think she was a little strange for making homemade meals for her bird, but as far as she was concerned, Cicero was a member of her family. Her parents had bought him as a six-month-old when she was just a baby, and he had been raised alongside her. With a fifty-year life span, he was currently only considered middle-aged by parrot standards, and would be with her for decades to come. He could even talk, though ear-piercing whistles seemed to be his current favorite way to communicate. He was a life-long fixture in her life, and she enjoyed spoiling him with healthy, fresh foods every day. Being able to afford the best for her pet was one of the many, many perks of having won millions through the lottery the year before.

Once Tulia's omelet was done, she eased it onto a plate, and then carried both her plate and Cicero's bowl out to the balcony. She opened the small side door and put his food dish in the bowl holder. While he climbed across the bars to reach it, she sat at the tiny, one-person wicker table next to his cage and took a sip of her cooling coffee before cutting into her omelet.

Loon Bay was a small town on the Atlantic coast,

not far from Boston. The town had a picturesque, New England feel that had charmed her as soon as she saw it, and the view of the coast from her little apartment's balcony was breathtaking. She had grown up in a state that boasted the largest freshwater lakes in the world but had never lived near the water before. She could hardly wait to add daily visits to the beach to her routine.

After breakfast was over and the dishes were washed, she got her things together, put on her shoes, and put Cicero's special avian harness on him. Then, with the bird perched on one hand, she stepped out the door and, just as she had done every day for the past five days, she set out down the street toward Samuel and Marc's office.

She wasn't an official employee there, but they had talked about adding her to the company in some way. She wasn't sure if she wanted to commit to getting her private investigator's license, but she had time to decide. This was just the start of the newest phase of her life. She had nothing but options.

Samuel and Marc were the only two in the office today; they had one other employee, but he was currently working from home—one of the benefits of his role as the tech expert. The office had a small wooden stand on a table in the corner for Cicero, and the bird had been there often enough during visits before they moved there that he flew directly over to it as soon as she was inside the building and detached the elastic leash from his harness.

Samuel rose from behind his desk and came over to give her a kiss in greeting. She smiled, still getting used to the fact that they were able to see each other every single day now. Making a long-distance relationship work had been difficult, but it had been worth the effort.

"Good morning," he said. "How was the rest of your day yesterday?"

"Good," she said. "I finally managed to give away the last of the moving boxes, and I had a nice video call with my parents. They said to say hi."

He smiled. "I'm glad they don't blame me for stealing their only daughter away."

"Oh, they do," she told him jokingly. "If they come out here to visit for Christmas, watch out for poison in the eggnog."

"Noted," he said with a chuckle.

"You know, I'm starting to realize Violet and I might have made you feel like the third wheel a time or two, Samuel," Marc cut in from behind his own desk across the room. "If that's the case, I should apologize. I *should*, mind you. I'm not going to, because you two are just as bad as we were when we first met."

"Sorry," Tulia said, giving Samuel one last peck on the cheek before moving over toward Marc's desk to say hello to him. He was smiling, and she knew he was mostly joking, but she also knew it probably wasn't very fun for him to be left sitting awkwardly while she and Samuel were wrapped up in each other.

Plus, even though it was just the two of them and they owned the business, they were technically at work.

"Oh, I forgot to tell you, Tulia," Samuel said as he returned to his own desk. "We got a call this morning from a woman who wanted to see us urgently. She'll be here in about twenty minutes."

"Oh? What does she want?"

He grimaced. "Her fiancé is missing, and she's worried."

Tulia winced. She'd heard about enough of their cases to know this one was likely to end in one of two ways. Either the woman's fiancé was genuinely in some sort of trouble, or he was having an affair or hiding some other sort of huge secret. Neither outcome would be good.

One of the negatives about the work Samuel and Marc did was that they saw a lot of the darker side of society. It was only the knowledge that their work was helping make the world a better place, and the thrill of solving a mystery, that made it worth it.

The three of them chatted until the new client's last-minute appointment time rolled around. She was punctual, opening the door right on time. Like most new clients Tulia had seen, she looked both hesitant and curious as she entered the office.

"Hi, I'm Amelia Stevens. I called earlier?"

"Come on in," Samuel said, rising to shake her hand. He directed her to the couch and offered her refreshments, then introduced himself, Marc, and Tulia before asking her to explain what she needed help with in more detail.

"Well, it all started about two weeks ago," Amelia said. She shot Cicero a curious look, but then refocused on her explanation. "My fiancé, Alan Casey, started acting a little strangely. Just small things—I noticed he stopped leaving on time for work and would get home at odd hours, he started taking me out to eat more often, buying me gifts… I thought it was all a little odd, but most of it was nice, and I wasn't too concerned until he went missing. And before you say he was probably cheating on me; no, he wasn't. Alan wouldn't do that."

Tulia saw Samuel and Marc exchange a look and

knew that they were reserving judgment on the woman's faith in her fiancé for the time being.

"So, he was acting strangely, then he went missing?" Marc prodded gently.

Amelia hesitated. "No … not exactly. Before you turn me down, hear me out, all right? I can pay. Whatever you need. The travel expenses won't be an issue."

"Travel expenses?" Samuel arched an eyebrow. "I admit, I'm curious."

She took a deep breath. "Four days ago, I drove Alan and one of his friends to the airport. He flew to Alaska to go on a last-minute hiking trip with some buddies from high school—he grew up in Anchorage. He was supposed to check in two days ago, but I haven't heard from him. I contacted the local authorities, but since they aren't expected back for another week, they won't do anything. This isn't the first time he's gone on a trip like this, and he *always* contacts me when he says he will. Between that and his strange behavior before going on the trip, I'm worried something bad happened. He could be in some sort of trouble. I need your help finding him."

Marc looked hesitant, but Samuel met Tulia's eyes. She wasn't yet at the same level of silent communication that he shared with Marc, but she thought she knew what he was asking. She gave a slight nod.

Yes, she definitely *was* interested in a last-minute trip to Alaska to find a missing man. She glanced at Cicero. She would just need to find someone to watch her bird.

"You said he traveled with a friend," Samuel said, reaching for a notepad. "Can you give me this friend's name? How did they know each other?"

"His name is Loren Sayers. They worked together back when Alan first moved here and have been close friends for years." She frowned. "They were out at a sports bar together the night I noticed Alan started acting strangely."

"Strangely how?" Samuel asked.

"It's hard to explain," she said. "He was just very … off when he came home later that night. Like I said, I didn't think much of it at the time, but combined with everything else … I'm concerned. I have the GPS coordinates of the campsite they like to hike out to. Oh, I do know at least one place they stopped in Anchorage if that would be helpful. It's a little outdoor supply store Alan likes…"

As Amelia started detailing the last known day of Alan's life, Tulia scrolled through her phone's contacts until she saw Violet's name. Marc's wife had become a good friend of hers, and if anyone was up for some last-minute bird-sitting duties, it would be her. She'd have to find some way to thank her, though if Tulia accompanying Samuel kept Marc at home with his wife, that might be payment enough for Violet. She had been understandably more concerned about her husband's choice of career after he had been shot on a case the year prior.

Tulia had been wanting to go to Alaska, and this seemed like the perfect chance. With a little luck, they would find Alan safe and sound right where he was supposed to be, and she and Samuel could spend the rest of their trip exploring the great outdoors.

CHAPTER TWO

Two business-class tickets to Anchorage charged to the private investigating firm's expenses account got Tulia and Samuel a last-minute, late-night flight to Anchorage. The suddenness of their trip made her head spin, but she felt the old excitement growing in her as they boarded the plane. The feeling faded a little during the boredom and discomfort of the ten-hour long flight—she was glad it was an overnight flight, since it meant she was able to sleep for most of it—but came back full force when they began their early-morning descent to the coastal city. Framed between the shining blue waters of the bay and a white-capped mountain range, it was one of the most beautiful sights she had ever seen.

They were traveling light, with only one carry-on

each. Since Alan went missing during a hike, Tulia knew she and Samuel were probably going to have to put their own wilderness skills to the test. She was a little excited at the prospect, which made her feel guilty—they were out here to find a missing man who may be hurt or in trouble, after all.

"Do you want to get breakfast, or head straight for the outdoor supply store?" Samuel asked once they were in their rental car. Tulia rolled the window down, eager to get more of a feel for the new state.

"Let's go straight to the store Amelia mentioned," Tulia said. "We can always grab breakfast on the way to wherever we go next. If he *is* in trouble, I don't want to be ten minutes too late to help him because we decided to grab some breakfast sandwiches first."

Samuel snorted. "If we're cutting it that close, I don't think the guy's chances are very good."

"*Do* you think he's in trouble?" she asked.

Once they decided to take the case and go to Alaska, most of their focus had been on arranging the trip, packing, and doing last-minute research since neither of them had actually been to the state before. Then they had been squished into a three-seat row with a stranger next to them, and it had made more sense to get some sleep than to try to talk privately on a plane full of listening ears. This was the first private moment they'd had to really discuss what they were here for.

"I doubt it," he said. "I think it's more likely that he's hiding something or feeling guilty about something, and she's picking up on that. But she's paying us to look into this, and this is what Marc and I are here for. We take the cases police won't or can't for some reason—as well as cases that have nothing to do with anything criminal in the first place."

"I feel a little bad if we're wasting her money," Tulia said as she put the store's address into her GPS. "If he's just too busy drinking and having fun with his friends and forgot to get in touch with her, she's going to be out what she's paying us on top of having a careless fiancé."

Tulia was getting paid as a contractor for this case, despite her objections. When she tried to argue that she really didn't need the money, Samuel had said something about their firm's insurance requiring everyone working on a case to be tied to a legal contract, which had pretty much stopped her objections in thcir tracks.

"A lot of our clients are relieved if we don't turn anything out of the ordinary up," he said as he started guiding the car out of the airport's parking lot. "I'm sure she would rather be out what she's paying us, than have us come back to her with the news that her fiancé is involved in drug trafficking or has a secret family."

"True," Tulia said with a wince. "Making calls to give your clients that sort of news must not be much fun."

"It's not," he said grimly. "So I really hope we find nothing except for a happy group of hikers when we get out there."

The store Amelia had told them about was called Ben's Adventure Supply and Wholesale, and it was on the northern edge of Anchorage in a building that looked more like a storehouse than a proper store. They went inside, and Tulia took a moment to look around, taking in the mounted taxidermy displays and fishing trophies.

"This place is huge," she murmured as they approached the front counter. "Amelia made it sound like a hole-in-the-wall place."

"She may have never been here," he pointed out. "We'll have to ask her if she ever went with him on any of these hiking trips."

The young man behind the counter looked bored, and watched their approach blankly, his phone in one hand. Tulia saw Samuel's lips twitch in a smile moments before he withdrew his PI badge from his jeans pocket.

"Samuel Noble, Private Investigator," he said as he showed the young man the badge. "I was wondering if you could help me."

Tulia smiled when his eyes lit up. She knew Samuel enjoyed the reaction he got out of people who were enthralled by the romanticized notion of being a private investigator. She would even admit that she had been a little starstruck herself, back when she first got to know him and Marc. Well, after realizing that they weren't actually stalkers out for her blood.

The day-to-day realities of the job had made her realize that like any other job, it had its ups and downs. She loved being involved with their work but had lost that starry-eyed reverence for the job sometime around when she saw exactly how much paperwork they had to do.

"Yeah, definitely. What's up?" the young man asked. He had a badge on his shirt that read *Ralph* but made no move to introduce himself.

"We're looking for a group who passed through this store a few days ago. Four guys and one woman," he said, repeating the information Amelia had given them about Alan's Alaskan friends. "They would have been planning on going on a week-long back-packing trip."

"That sounds like almost every customer we have," Ralph said. "I'm going to need more than that."

"One should have had a Massachusetts driver's license," Samuel said.

"Oh, I remember them," Ralph said, sitting up straighter. "He had to show it to me to get a nonresident fishing license. Did they commit a crime? You know, I almost had to call the cops on them."

Tulia's eyebrows rose. She still felt a little unsure about joining in when Samuel was questioning someone, but she *was* getting paid for this. She might as well try to pull her own weight.

"Really? What did they do?" she asked.

"The Massachusetts guy and another guy got into an argument. It was pretty bad—I thought they were going to start throwing punches until the two other guys they were with pulled them apart."

"Do you remember what the other man involved in the argument looked like?" Samuel asked.

"Ah, he had brown hair and looked like he got a lot of sun. He was tall, too. Taller than you."

"Thanks," Samuel said as Tulia made a note about

it on her phone. "Did you happen to hear what the argument was about?"

"Not really. I was more worried about them fighting than about eavesdropping. But it sounded like the Massachusetts guy broke a promise or something."

Tulia was thoroughly intrigued. "Did they say anything about where they were going?"

Amelia had seemed certain she knew their destination, but there was no telling what Alan was hiding from her. It could be nothing, or it could be something major.

"Ah, they were starting out from a pretty popular area about forty miles north of here," Ralph said. "They were going to do some backcountry hiking, I think. They didn't mention anything any more specific than that. They got a tent, some fishing gear, and a few other normal camping items. I could probably find their receipts, if you two want a copy of them."

"Perfect," Samuel said. "We appreciate it. While you're at it, what supplies would you recommend for two people interested in following them?"

Ralph's grin turned predatory. "Two newbies when it comes to the Alaskan wilderness, huh? Well, you're in luck. Here at Ben's Adventure Supply and

Wholesale, we sell everything you could possibly need. Follow me, and grab a cart. I'll get you two hooked up."

Tulia had a feeling Ralph was about to make his biggest sale all month.

CHAPTER THREE

"I'm still not sure the satellite phone was necessary," Tulia muttered, turning the heavy device over in her hands.

"It's probably overkill, but given the circumstances of why Amelia hired us, we have reason to believe that there's a possibility Alan might be injured or in some sort of trouble. We aren't going to get any cell service out there, so if we need to make an emergency call, we'll be glad we have it." He grimaced. "I'm still not convinced this man is in danger, but I'm beginning to be a little more convinced that something is going on. I'd rather not regret not buying it."

They were on their way to the popular trailhead north of Anchorage that Ralph had mentioned, because it lined up with what Amelia had told them about where Alan was going to be. In addition to the satellite phone and the myriad of other supplies they would need to safely hike and overnight in the Alaskan wilderness, they had purchased a GPS device that was a lot more robust than Tulia's cell phone was. Samuel had his notes on the case stored on his phone, so Tulia scrolled through the app until she saw the coordinates that Amelia had supplied them with. She typed them into the GPS device, then looked through the instructions the device had come with to figure out how to set a pin at their current location. She intended to set a pin wherever they ended up leaving their car, so they could find their way back if they got lost.

It was midday by the time they pulled off the road onto a bumpy dirt path. Ralph's instructions had been accurate so far, but it wasn't until they had gone nearly half a mile down the path and saw a muddy off-road SUV parked on a flat patch of grass that they knew for sure they were in the right place.

"I'm glad we stopped at the store," Samuel said as he parked next to the SUV. "Ralph was a lot more helpful than I expected."

He was the one who had given them the description of the vehicle Alan's group had driven away in. It was only thanks to him that they knew they were on the right track.

"Hopefully, we keep getting lucky," Tulia said as she unbuckled her seatbelt. "If they aren't at the coordinates Amelia gave us, we are going to be out of luck unless your skills as a private investigator include tracking someone through the wilderness."

"Funnily enough, they didn't include that on my test."

She snorted as she swung her legs out of the car and walked around to the trunk to get her things. She tucked the GPS device securely into the side pocket of her backpack, then looked through the car again to double check that she wasn't forgetting anything. They had bought a lot of supplies, along with an Alaskan wilderness survival guide, and the satellite phone, which they could use to call for help if they got into trouble. They were probably more prepared than a lot of people who went hiking out here, but Tulia was still nervous.

She had done her share of hiking and camping, but this felt different. This wasn't a designated campground with neatly groomed trails, nor was it one of the popular, widely recommended spots she had researched to camp out with her RV when she was on state land out West. This was true wilderness. The sort that people could disappear in.

She only hoped Alan wasn't one of those people.

Samuel hit a button on the key fob, and the car locked with a beep. The two of them hesitated for a moment, then Samuel cleared his throat.

"Well, we had better get going. It will take us a few hours to reach the spot Amelia told us about. We'll want to get there before dark."

In other circumstances, the hike might have been fun. The scenery was gorgeous. Alaska's summer might have been short, but it was breathtakingly beautiful. The air was fresh and clean, and the sky was a pure blue, without a cloud in sight. She could have done without the bugs, but bug spray was one of the many supplies they had picked up at the store. She and Samuel didn't talk much, saving their energy for hiking instead. They made decent progress, pausing every once in a while to check the GPS to make sure they were still heading in the right direction.

They stopped for a short break a few hours in and took in the view. A winding river was just visible in the distance, miles away, and she knew their destination lay somewhere along its banks.

The sun was hanging low in the sky by the time they neared the coordinates Amelia had given them.

They slowed down and started to scan the area for any signs of a camp. They were almost on top of it before they saw it; they crested a hill that fell off in a sheer, rocky cliff on the other side. Nestled in the valley between it and another hill was a campsite with four tents set up in a semicircle around a fire pit.

"That has to be them," Samuel muttered.

Tulia hiked her backpack up, feeling tired down to her bones. "I don't see anyone, though. Do you?"

He frowned, raising a hand to shield his eyes from the evening sun as he squinted down into the valley.

"No, I don't. Let's go see what's going on."

They carefully descended the rocky hillside and approached the camp. The smell of smoke lingered on the air—they must have had the fire going earlier that day. As they neared, Samuel called out, "Hello?" but no one responded. The campsite remained eerily still.

"This is creepy," Tulia whispered as they stepped into the semicircle of tents. "Where is everyone?"

"They might be out on a hike," he pointed out. "Or fishing. We know they got fishing licenses."

His words made her relax a little. He was right. These people had come out here to enjoy nature, not just sit around a campsite all day.

"So, what should we do?" she asked. "Just wait here until they get back?"

"I suppose," he said. "It's not as if we could track them down. Maybe we should take a little peek around the campsite while we wait. We won't mess with anyone's belongings, but it can't hurt to see what's here."

Snooping Tulia could handle. She set her heavy backpack down by the fire pit, stretched her aching back, then started wandering around the campsite. A few folding chairs were set up near the fire, and a clean cooking pot was sitting atop of one of them. There were plenty of signs people had been using the campsite up until recently. She could see some footprints and scuffs in the softer parts of the ground, and someone had strung a makeshift laundry line up between two of the tents. A few shirts were drying on it.

She was walking past one of the tents when she noticed the little flap that covered the screen window in the door hadn't been zipped up all the way. She paused and crouched down to peer into it, figuring it wouldn't hurt anything if she just looked. What she saw made her eyes widen.

"Hello?" she called out, raising her voice slightly. "Are you okay?"

There was no response from the still form she saw

lying inside the tent. She straightened up and waved Samuel over.

"Someone's inside this tent, and they aren't moving."

He frowned and peered through the screen, then started to unzip the tent's door. He pushed his way inside and Tulia followed, stooping to keep her head from brushing the top of the tent. There was an unpleasant smell inside, the sight of the human form made her breath catch in her throat. It had been hard to see through the screen, but now she saw that the form had a sheet pulled over their body. It lay there, unmoving, as Samuel knelt beside it. Slowly, he reached down and pulled the sheet away from the person's face.

Tulia recognized Alan Casey's face from the photograph Amelia had given them. And he definitely wasn't sleeping. He was very, very dead.

CHAPTER FOUR

The sound of voices in the distance caught Tulia's attention, and she backed out of the tent. Samuel paused to re-cover the dead man's face and then followed her. He stood next to her, his arms crossed. She could tell how tense he was just by looking at his face. She felt a similar tension in her own body, along with a cold knot in her stomach. Alan was dead. The man they had been hired to find was dead, which meant they had been too late.

He was dead, and the group of people who might be responsible for his death were on their way back.

"Follow my lead," said Samuel. "We don't know how he died. Don't accuse anyone of anything no matter what you think. If it *wasn't* accidental, we could be in trouble."

She nodded, her jaw clenched tightly. Soon, the first person appeared over the hill. A man, with a fishing pole over one shoulder and a rope with a fish stringed on it in the other hand. Two other men and a woman followed him.

They paused as a group when they saw Tulia and Samuel standing in front of Alan's tent. She could see the sudden uncertainty that went through the group before the man at the front of the group raised a hand in a wave and approached them. He was walking with a limp, she noticed. He looked a little older than the others, with some grey in his beard and short, unwashed hair. His face was tanned and deeply lined, and he looked like someone who spent a lot of time working outside.

"Are you two lost?" he asked, his voice gruff.

Samuel shook his head. "Far from it. We are right where we need to be." He reached into his pocket to take out his wallet and flipped it open to show his ID. "I'm Samuel Noble, a private investigator, and this is my partner, Tulia. We were hired to find a missing man."

"We haven't seen anyone else around here," the older man said.

"Funny, because the body we found in the tent behind us seems to argue otherwise," Samuel bit out.

The man's jaw clenched, but then he seemed to slump. "You're here for Alan. Why didn't you just say so? I didn't think anyone had reported him missing yet."

The admission seemed to snap the other people out of their shock. Slowly, they all approached Samuel and Tulia as well. The woman, who looked to be closest to the older man in age, slipped her arm through his.

"You're private investigators?" she asked, her eyes curious as she looked them over. "I'm Carolyn Grant, and this is my husband, John. We've known Alan since he was just a boy. His fiancée was the one who hired you, wasn't she? Amelia?"

"The identity of my client is confidential," Samuel said. "Can I get the rest of your names?"

"I'm Robert Newsom," a man who matched the description Ralph had given them said. He was tall— the tallest in the group. Like Alan, he looked to be in his early thirties. "I've known Alan almost my entire life. We met in middle school and were close all the way through our first two years of college, when Alan moved out to the East Coast to finish up his degree."

"Loren Sayers," the last man said. Tulia remembered the name—Amelia had mentioned it. He was Alan's best friend in the Boston area. He looked less in his element than the others, with slicked back dirty-blonde hair and clothing that looked more expensive than functional. "I flew out here with Alan for the trip. I have no idea how I'm going to tell Amelia what happened."

"What *did* happen?" Tulia asked. All four of them looked tired and worn out. John had that limp, and Carolyn was rubbing her temples as if she had a headache. None of them looked like killers.

John grimaced. "Food poisoning. That has to be it. It was about two days after we got out here. We all ate dinner together, and we started getting sick later that night. We didn't realize until late the next morning that Alan had passed away in his tent. We aren't sure why he was the one who was hit the hardest. He must've had an underlying condition that we weren't aware of."

"I'm the only one who didn't get sick. I'm a vegetarian," Carolyn told them. "I brought all my own food and prepared it separately. We threw out everything the guys ate, which is why we've been going fishing for food."

"Why haven't you sent anyone back to get help?" Samuel asked. "It's been, what, three days since he passed away? It's less than a day's hike back to your vehicle."

"We just started feeling better today," John said. "It might not be that long of a hike, but I didn't want anyone to move away from the river until the symptoms had passed. Dehydration can set in quickly when you're sick, and it's my job to keep the rest of these people safe." At their confused looks, he added, "While I'm personal friends with everyone here, I also work as a professional Alaskan wilderness tour guide."

"Were you planning on hiking back tonight, since you're feeling better?"

"Tomorrow," John said. "I rolled my ankle earlier that same evening we all got sick. It should be good enough for me to make the hike tomorrow."

"One more night out here," Carolyn said with a shudder. "I'll be so glad when this is over."

John wrapped an arm around her. Behind them, Robert sat in a chair by the fire, grabbed a flat wooden board, and started cleaning the fish. Loren crouched near the fire and started to rekindle it.

"I'm not surprised Amelia guessed something was wrong," he said once he had a small flame going. "She didn't want him to go on this trip in the first place."

"I know the dangers of being out here better than

anyone," John murmured. "But I never thought something like this could happen on my watch."

It was far too late for Samuel and Tulia to start going back to their car tonight. They decided to set up camp on the opposite side of the fire from the other tents. The rest of the group gave them their blessing to do so, and Tulia and Samuel worked together to get the tent set up and their sleeping rolls laid out inside of it. It looked cozy enough, but the canvas walls didn't offer much in the way of privacy. They decided to take a walk up the hill together, and away from the smell of cooking fish and the crackling fire with only their flashlights to guide them.

Once they were at the top of the hill and could see all of the others still gathered around the fire, they sat down on a rocky outcropping.

"Do you think they're telling the truth?" she whispered to Samuel, cautious of her voice carrying.

"I'm not sure," he responded quietly. "It's possible. But I noticed something odd in their story. Carolyn wasn't sick, and she's John's wife. It's only six or so hours back to their SUV, and it seems like easy enough terrain. You would think that if all of them were violently ill and one of them was dead, the only healthy person—who happens to be married to a wilderness guide and probably knows a lot about survival herself—would've gone back to get help. So, why didn't she?"

Tulia looked down at the fire and the people gathered around it. It was a good question, and one that hadn't occurred to her. It did seem a little odd that they had waited three days with a corpse instead of finding a way to get help. Six hours might have been a long hike under normal circumstances, but it certainly seemed preferable to waiting out here with the body of one of their friends tucked away inside a tent.

"Do you think they're *all* hiding something?"

He shrugged. "It's a possibility. We have to be careful. If they're in on this together, this could become very dangerous for us very quickly."

CHAPTER FIVE

Tulia might have been a little spoiled by her long trip in her top-of-the-line RV. This was far from the first time she had slept in a tent, but it had been nearly half a year since she had gone camping, and back then, she had never been very far away from the creature comforts her RV offered.

She woke up early in the morning with an aching back and the irritating sensation of everything being just slightly damp from the dew that had gathered on the tent during the night.

This was *real* camping   there were no showers or bathrooms, not even a porta potty with a hole in the ground. After climbing out of the tent quietly so as not to disturb Samuel, she used some of the water they had brought to brush her teeth and then sat on one of the camp chairs by the fire pit and did her best to get herself feeling presentable with the help of her tiny pocket mirror and a small hairbrush.

As she was putting her supplies back into her toiletry bag, the soft sound of a footstep in the dew-damp grass made her turn around. It was just Samuel, and she released a breath she hadn't been aware she was holding. She wasn't sure what she had expected to find out here, but it certainly hadn't been a group of potential murder suspects, and she was on edge because of it.

"We should pack up and get ready to go soon," he told her quietly. "Even if the rest of this group doesn't want to leave this early, there's no reason we can't head back ourselves and alert the authorities."

The fact that it might be safer for them to return to civilization alone together rather than traveling with the group went unsaid.

"Do you think we should call the authorities with that satellite phone?" she asked, keeping her voice low. "I don't know why I didn't think of it last night, I guess I was just too distracted with everything else."

"I tried to when I woke up this morning, but the signal was too spotty."

She frowned. "Aren't they supposed to work anywhere?"

"It needs to be able to connect with the satellite relay. I think the fact that we are in a valley is keeping the signal from getting through. If we hike up to the top of the hill, we should be able to get a signal."

"Okay, let's do that first, then," she said. "Then we can head back—"

She broke off at the sound of a tent unzipping. It was Loren Sayers, Alan's friend from Massachusetts. He looked like he had hardly slept, and he rubbed his eyes as he climbed out of the tent. But when his gaze focused on them, it was sharp and clear. He looked around, seemed to note that no one else was up yet, then started walking away from the campsite. He paused after a few feet and turned to look at them, then jerked his head in a silent motion that encouraged them to follow him.

A little puzzled, Tulia glanced at Samuel, who raised an eyebrow but nodded before helping her to her feet.

They followed Loren out of the campsite and closer to the river, far enough that when he stopped and turned around to speak to them, there was no chance of the others overhearing.

"If Amelia hired a private investigator, she must have had a reason to think Alan was in some sort of trouble," he said, keeping his voice low. "What did she say?"

Samuel frowned. "I don't believe I ever confirmed that Alan's fiancée was the one who hired us, and I'm not at liberty to discuss a private conversation I've had with my client."

Loren sighed, sounding irritated and at the end of his rope.

"Look, it has to have been her. You don't have to confirm it, but I'm just going to go ahead and assume it was. She noticed he was acting odd, didn't she? Well, there was a reason for that, and I'm worried it might have something to do with his death."

Tulia and Samuel exchanged a look. This time, it was Tulia who spoke up. "So he didn't die of food poisoning?"

"I don't have any proof," Loren said. "But things were … tense." He took a deep breath. "Two weeks before he went on this trip, Alan won the lottery."

Surprise made Tulia's eyes widen. She barely kept from blurting out that she had won a lottery too, and instead she kept her lips pressed tight together. Thankfully, Samuel didn't give anything away either.

"Was it a significant amount?"

Loren nodded. "Quite significant. I was with him

when he realized he won, so I was the first person to know about it."

"And he didn't tell his fiancée? That's why she noticed he was acting oddly, but didn't know why?"

"Exactly," Loren said. "He wanted some time to think over what he was going to do first. We talked about it on the flight, and he told me he was going to surprise her with the news when he got back, though I think I had convinced him to also look into doing a prenup before they got married. Anyway, while we were picking up some supplies after meeting up with everyone in Anchorage, I let it slip that he had won the lottery. He was looking at a new tent and said something about how pricey it was, and I said something about how he didn't have to worry about that anymore, what with his winning ticket. Robert overheard. He and Alan got into a big argument while we were at the store, and we almost got kicked out.

He sighed and ran a hand through his hair before continuing.

"Somehow, Carolyn and John found out too. The whole thing was a mess. Everyone started acting oddly toward him before we even got to the campsite, which was exactly what he didn't want." He took a deep breath. "Trust me when I say I feel horrible that I'm the reason everyone found out. I don't know exactly what happened, but I'm pretty sure both Robert and Carolyn asked him for money at different points. Then he just drops dead after a little food poisoning? That doesn't make sense to me. Everyone was acting so strangely, and tensions were running so high, my gut told me right away he had been murdered, even though we didn't see any injuries on him. I've been trying to stall our return in the hope I could figure out who killed him and how. But now that you're here, maybe you can help. I know Amelia…" He rolled his eyes. "Or *whoever* hired you might not have paid you enough for this, but you're here anyway. Will you help me figure out the truth?"

"We'll keep our eyes peeled," Samuel promised. "Thank you for telling us all of that."

Loren nodded and started heading back toward the campsite. Tulia and Samuel lingered at a distance so they could have another brief, private conversation.

"What do you think?" Tulia murmured as she watched Loren head back toward the tents.

"The fact that he won the lottery is certainly new and might change some things," Samuel said. "But I'm not sure I buy that Loren has been trying to delay the return so he can solve the case himself. Why not go to the police, if he was worried Alan's death was a homicide? Keeping the authorities from being able to investigate the body will only make the medical examiner's job more difficult, as decomposition begins to set in."

"I didn't even think of that," she said with a frown. "But why tell us all of that if he wasn't being honest?"

"Maybe he was, maybe he wasn't. I just don't want to get too comfortable with anyone here." He gave her a small smile. "I'm glad you didn't tell any of the wrong people about *your* lottery winnings."

"That's exactly why I've been so careful," she said. "You know I'm not a superstitious person, but all the research I did when I won makes me think there's some sort of curse on lottery winners. So many of them end up destitute or dead after they win the lottery. I hope we can find justice for Alan. He deserved better than this."

CHAPTER SIX

As they walked back to the campsite, the others in the camp began stirring. Carolyn started making coffee over the coals of last night's fire, and John followed her out of their tent a moment later, stretching and giving a loud yawn. That seemed to wake Robert up, and by the time she and Samuel reached their tent, the entire camp was awake and active.

"Oh, are you leaving already?" Carolyn asked, looking up from the metal pot of coffee as Samuel handed Tulia her backpack from inside the tent. She slipped it over her shoulders as the warm, familiar scent of coffee began to spread through the air.

She really wished she had thought to bring some, even if it was just the instant stuff. It was tempting to ask Carolyn for a cup, but bumming a cup of coffee off of someone who might be involved in a murder didn't sit quite right with her.

"We're just going for a quick walk up the hill," Tulia said.

"Taking in the sights, huh?" John said, coming up behind his wife to rub her shoulders.

"Neither of us have ever been to Alaska before," Samuel said. Neither of them wanted to bring up the satellite phone, in case someone in this camp wanted to keep Alan's death a secret.

"Well, in that case, why don't you take Carolyn with you?" He squeezed his wife's shoulder. "She knows this area almost as well as I do. What do you say, sweetie? I think a nice walk would cheer you up."

"Oh, all right," Carolyn said, leaving the metal pot sitting in the coals to continue heating up as she rose to her feet. "I suppose I could do with a stretch of my legs. I'd be happy to give you two a quick tour."

Tulia glanced at Samuel. She couldn't think of a good way to politely decline Carolyn's offer to join them, and it didn't seem Samuel could either, which meant they were going to have to use the satellite phone in front of her.

"We appreciate it," Samuel said after a beat. "I'll grab my bag, then we'll let you lead the way."

Carolyn knew an easier path back up the rocky hill than the one they had taken down the day before. She kept up a steady stream of chatter as she led them up the path. They were almost at the top when the subject of Alan came up.

"Sorry if the two of you wanted to get away for a private moment," she said. "But John was right. I needed to get away from that campsite. I know there isn't much we could do about it, but knowing Alan's body has been lying in that tent for days now is just so grim. He grew up right down the road from us. John was just getting into wilderness tours when his family moved in, and soon he started working for John's company in the summers. He was a good kid —though I guess he and his friends aren't exactly kids any longer. I still can't believe he's gone. And food poisoning, of all things."

"We didn't know him, but I agree that it's a shame," Samuel said. "And right after he won the lottery, too."

One of Tulia's eyebrows quirked. She hadn't been expecting Samuel to bring that up, but she listened closely to Carolyn's reply.

"Oh, someone told you about that?" Carolyn

asked. "I was so happy for him when I heard about it. Just imagine, winning the lottery…" She paused in her steps, her eyes going distant. "We could pay off medical bills, and I could convince John to retire early…" She shook her head. "What terrible luck, though. And the worst part is he only took this trip *because* he won that lottery drawing. He was so happy to be able to quit his job and could finally afford to be able to a last-minute trip like this."

She sighed and started walking again, leading them to the top of the hill. Up there, they all stopped, and Carolyn turned around slowly, taking in the view.

"I will never get tired of how beautiful it is out here," she said. "The two of you came at a good time. All those flowers you see, they'll be gone in just a couple of weeks. You should come back another time, when you can relax and enjoy the trip. There isn't anywhere quite like Alaska."

"It is beautiful," Tulia murmured. She slipped her backpack off and stooped to grab a bottle of water from inside of it but kept her eyes on the view.

Off to their left, the river curved around in a bend, its waters glimmering in the sunlight. The terrain was mostly open, with rolling hills and the occasional scraggly tree, and plenty of tall grasses and wildflowers. The mountains towered over the landscape off in the distance, the peaks still capped with snow. She felt like she was in a painting.

"If you'll excuse us for a second," Samuel said as he dropped his own backpack to the ground and unzipped it. "We need to make a call. As much as I would love to enjoy the view for longer, we're still on the clock. I need to call this in."

Carolyn's eyes widened as he took the satellite phone out.

"Oh! That's why you wanted to come up here. You're going to call your client?"

He shook his head. "Were calling the local authorities. Hopefully, they'll have some advice on what to do next."

The cat was out of the bag as far as the satellite phone went, but maybe it would be a good thing. If there was a killer in the group, now they would know that the authorities were aware of what was going on. Maybe caution would prevent them from doing anything further.

Tulia and Carolyn waited while Samuel made the call. Thankfully, the satellite phone got enough signal to work at the top of the hill, though it took a few tries for Samuel to get the information across. Finally, with a nod and a final "Will do," he ended the call.

"They'll have someone out here within forty-eight

hours," he said. "Possibly sooner, but it sounds like there's a storm coming in, and depending on exactly where it hits, it might delay them."

"Would we have time to get back before the storm comes?" Tulia asked.

He shook his head. "The ranger I spoke to suggested we all stay here. I told them one man has a twisted ankle and the others are recovering from food poisoning. He thinks it's best if we all just batten down and wait for the team of rescuers to arrive."

She tried not to let her displeasure show on her face. Forty-eight hours? It wasn't that she was upset about being in Alaska for longer than she had expected, but she wasn't thrilled with the thought of spending the next two days with this group of strangers she didn't trust.

"Well," Carolyn said, a forced-looking smile on her face. "That's that, then. Let's give the others the news. We'll have to figure out what to do about rations. I take it you brought your own supplies?"

Tulia and Samuel started figuring out how they were going to ration their supplies while they walked back down the hill, Carolyn chiming in occasionally with suggestions. Tulia's mind wasn't on that, though. It wasn't even on the upcoming two-day stay in the middle of nowhere.

Her thoughts were still stuck on the fact that Alan had won the lottery just before he died. Even though she had never met the man, somehow that single similarity between them made this case feel far too personal.

CHAPTER SEVEN

Carolyn spread the news of their call to the authorities when they got back to camp. No one responded with anything other than grim acceptance. John cast a wary look toward the still-clear skies.

"We'd better get this camp cleaned up and everything tied down if a storm is going to hit. It's a good thing the two of you had that satellite phone. I wouldn't want to be caught out on our way back to the road. I checked the weather before we left, and it was supposed to be clear, but these things can change."

"What are we going to do about food?" Carolyn asked. "They brought a little, and it will last them another two days if they only eat small meals, but they're going to run out of water, and no one is going to want to make the hike back on an empty stomach. It'll be too dangerous to get water from the river if it's a big storm."

"We'll have to get more water before the storm hits," John said. "We can try to fish more too. Loren, how about you go with the two newcomers to that same fishing spot we went to yesterday. Fill some of our empty containers with water, but remember we have to filter and boil it before we can drink it. See if you can catch any fish. I know we're all getting tired of it, but if we share some fish for dinner with these two, maybe they'll share some of what they brought, and we can all have a good meal tonight before the storm."

"Sure," Tulia said. "We'd be happy to share. "

"And happy to haul some water back too," Samuel said. "Lead the way."

Loren nodded. He grabbed his fishing pole, and all three of them took some of the empty water containers Robert, John, and Carolyn handed them, and then they set off in the opposite direction she and Samuel had gone to make the call with the satellite phone.

"Sorry that John's putting you to work," Loren said. "He's got a bad habit of thinking he can tell people what to do."

"It's fine," Tulia said. "He's the most experienced one when it comes to all of this survival stuff, and at least this way everyone's working together. Do storms get really bad out here?"

Loren shrugged. "I'm not sure. I've only been out here two other times with Alan. It rained a couple of times, but I never saw a really bad storm."

"Hopefully, it passes us by," Samuel said.

"I'm sorry you guys are stuck out here now," Loren sighed. "You probably weren't expecting to spend this long camping out. Did you call Amelia after you called the authorities?"

"I still haven't confirmed she's my client," Samuel said. "But no, I haven't alerted my client yet. We wanted to tell everyone about the storm and not to head out yet. If we have time, we'll find somewhere the satellite phone can connect from when we get back, and I'll get an update to her then."

"Since you brought up Amelia," Tulia said, giving voice to something that she had been curious about, "I was wondering if you had any idea why Alan was so reluctant to tell her he won the lottery? If they were already engaged, you'd think he would trust her with it."

"He wanted time to figure everything out," Loren said. "Alan has always been a cautious decision maker. I don't think it was that he didn't trust Amelia, he just wanted to figure out what he wanted to do with the money before he started getting other people's opinions about it, if that made sense. I wouldn't have known myself, if I hadn't been with him when he won. Here we are. You'll want to wade out into the river a little to get the cleanest water possible. And take water upstream of where you're standing, so the sediment you stir up doesn't go into the container."

The three of them took off their shoes and socks and spent some time filling up all the water containers. The walk back to camp would be a lot more difficult with the extra weight, but if a bad storm *did* hit, she was sure they would be glad for this effort.

Afterward, she and Samuel found a pair of large rocks to sit on while Loren fished. It would have been a peaceful scene if not for the knowledge that there was a dead man back at camp. Between the sound of the river and the distance between them and Loren, Tulia was certain he wouldn't be able to overhear her. Keeping her voice low, she said, "What are you going to tell Amelia about what happened?"

"The truth," Samuel said. "She hired us to find Alan, and she deserves to know what we found. It's not going to be a pleasant conversation, but it's the right thing to do."

"I mean, are you going to tell her about the food poisoning story, or about the lottery and the suspicion that foul play might have been involved in his death?"

He considered his answer for a moment. "I'm not sure. I think for now I'll tell her he is deceased, it's likely it was an accident, and that we're going to have to wait for the authorities to get involved for any further information. But I'm tempted to bring up the lottery, just to see what her response is. I also want to get more information on his friendship with Loren."

She looked at the man in question. He was reeling a struggling fish in, a scene that could have been in any nature magazine, though he still looked more like a city slicker than a mountain man.

He was the one who had come to them with information about the lottery, information he hadn't had to share. He was the one who had first drawn their notice toward the possibility of Alan's death being a homicide instead of an accident.

The logical part of her said he wouldn't do any of that if he was involved in what happened. Without the information he gave them, she and Samuel wouldn't have known anything at all about the entire lottery fiasco.

But she couldn't help but wonder exactly what had transpired between him and Alan when Alan first noticed he had a winning ticket. Had he insisted some of the money should be his? Had he tried to get his friend to share? Tulia was pretty sure any of her old friends from before her trip would have been quick to pounce on any money she won, especially if they saw her winning. It was one of the reasons she had kept it quiet from everyone except her parents.

From the sound of things, Alan wasn't the type to spend money quickly or impulsively, so she had to believe that if Loren had asked him to share his winnings, Alan wouldn't have been quick to agree.

As she watched Loren cast his line into the river, she wondered how he had felt about one of his best friends winning the lottery. He acted like it was nothing, but Tulia knew firsthand how much the thought of easy money could change people.

CHAPTER EIGHT

They returned to camp after Loren caught three more large fish. He caught a few smaller ones in between, which he released back into the river. Neither she nor Samuel had bought fishing poles or fishing licenses at the store they stopped at after landing in Anchorage, so they were relegated to watching. She didn't mind, though. At least she and Samuel were still contributing to the meal. They had brought a lot of dried foods, though they were more snack-like than meal-like. She really was happy to share, mostly because she was already getting sick of eating the dried food and was looking forward to something fresh.

The fish and their snacks made for a decent lunch. Carolyn and John cooked after Robert cleaned the fish, and while the meal was sizzling over the fire, he and Loren dragged some old logs over for her and Samuel to sit on.

The meal was mostly silent, everyone too lost in their own thoughts to make conversation. Tulia was beginning to wonder if Loren was wrong, and Alan's death really had been an accident. Everyone in the group seemed to be just as mournful as she would expect for someone who had lost a good friend in such an unexpected and unfair way.

But they were here as private investigators, which meant they couldn't just follow their feelings. They needed evidence.

Their discussion about Amelia seemed to have rekindled Samuel's drive to get to the truth of what happened to Alan. When Robert offered to take their dishes to the river to wash them after the meal, he volunteered to go too, and Tulia tagged along after them, carrying a small stack of dirty plates.

"Okay, what is it?" Robert asked as he bent his long legs to crouch next to the river and began scrubbing the cooking pot clean with a handful of sand. "I'm guessing the two of you followed me out here to have a private talk with me, like you already did with Carolyn and Loren."

Tulia frowned. It hadn't been like that, not really. They hadn't even wanted Carolyn to go with them when they made the call on the satellite phone, and Loren had been the one to approach *them* for a private talk. But in retrospect, she could see why it looked that way to him.

"I did want to talk to you," Samuel said. "But if you're not comfortable with it, I'm happy to just wash the dishes and go back. My questions aren't about his death, exactly. It's about something else that's been bothering me."

"Ask what you want to ask," Robert said. "I don't have anything to hide." He seemed defensive to Tulia, but she focused on scrubbing the dishes she had carried out here, not comfortable with chiming in since she wasn't sure yet where Samuel wanted to go with this conversation.

"A couple of people mentioned that you got into a serious argument with Alan at the store you stopped at before coming out here," Samuel began. "Can you tell me what that was about?"

"It was hardly serious," Robert said with a scoff. "He just took a joke the wrong way, that's all."

"Weren't you friends with him for, like, your whole life?" Tulia asked. It seemed strange to her that such an old friend could take an offhanded joke so poorly as to start a public argument that almost got them kicked out of a store.

"We've gotten more distant in the last few years." Robert sighed. "It was… Well, you know he won a lot of money in the lottery, right? Back when we were eighteen, we both got into buying lottery tickets with every paycheck, and we made a promise that if one of us won, he would split the winnings with the other. When Loren said something about Alan winning a lot of money, I jokingly asked Alan if he was still planning on splitting it with me, and he completely lost it. He's the one who started the argument, if anything."

"I see," Samuel said. "It sounds like it was just a misunderstanding."

"Yeah. If *I* had won, I would've shared it with him," Robert muttered, scrubbing the pot more violently. "So what if it's been over a decade since we made that promise? He was still one of my best friends. But he didn't need to jump down my throat about it, he could've just said no. I guess it's true that money changes people."

He splashed the pot into the river, rinsing it off. Tulia quickly rinsed off her own plates, while Samuel worked on the tin cups and the flatware.

Tulia was tempted to say something about her own experience with winning the lottery, but she wasn't sure she wanted to bring it up. Not now. Not when the question of why Alan really died was still up in the air, and not after hearing how Alan's friends had all started pestering him for money as soon as they learned he had hit the jackpot.

They didn't talk much more as they finished cleaning off the dishes, and soon they started the walk back to the camp. Tulia frowned as they came over the hill and she spotted John hefting a large backpack onto his back.

"Is he leaving?" she asked. "I thought we had all agreed to stay."

"No way is he going back to the vehicle and leaving all of us here," Robert snapped. "Either we all stay, or we all go. We need him if that storm hits."

It seemed Robert wasn't the only one who disagreed with him leaving. As they got closer, they heard the sound of an argument. Soon, Tulia could make out the words.

"We all agreed to camp here until the storm is over," Loren was saying. "I don't get why the two of you changed your mind so suddenly. We need you here."

"I'm worried this valley we're in might flood if the storm is bad enough," John said. "It's not supposed to hit until tomorrow anyway. I can go into town, get a good look at the weather forecast, and if it looks as bad as Samuel said, we'll get some people with all-terrain vehicles and come back here to help everyone get out of here."

"You'll be fine," Carolyn said. Tulia realized she had a backpack sitting by her feet and looked ready to go. "John and I will be a lot faster alone than all six of us trying to go at once, and I know none of us want to leave Alan's body here on its own."

"Hey," Robert called out as they strode into the campsite. "I'm with Loren on this. You can't go. Not just because we need you here, but it's afternoon already. You're going to get caught out at night, and we don't know exactly when the storm is going to hit. I heard what Samuel said, and it sounded like it could be anytime between now and this time tomorrow. It's a bad idea. I'm surprised at you, John. You should know better."

"I know how dangerous it can be to get caught out here in a storm, especially so close to a river," John retorted. "Carolyn pointed out that we could be in trouble, and I agree with her, but we have no good way to move Alan's body without vehicles."

"But it's riskier to get caught in a storm without any shelter," Robert pointed out. "The authorities have our coordinates, so even if we run into trouble, they'll be able to find us. We'll keep an eye on the conditions, and if it looks like it's going to flood, we can move onto one of the hills for safety. But if you go out there and your ankle slows you down, and you get caught out overnight, and the storm hits before sunrise, no one is going to have a clue where to find you."

John hesitated, looking uncertain. He was the most experienced one out here, and Tulia knew pride could come along with that sort of experience. He might know the risks, but he thought he was able to beat them.

"John, I don't want to be out here another night," Carolyn said, her voice shaking part way through the sentence. "I can't do it."

"My ankle is still bothering me, Carolyn," John said after a moment, his shoulders slumping. "Robert's right. There's a good chance we can make it back to the SUV and everything will be fine, but if something happens out there, we're going to be in a lot more trouble than we would be if we just stay here. We'll wait until morning, and as long as the weather holds, we'll leave at first light."

Carolyn didn't look happy with the proclamation, but she didn't argue as she carried her backpack back into the tent. John took his own pack off, letting it drop to the ground next to the fire pit, and Tulia and Samuel were finally able to hand the dishes over to Loren, who put them away.

None of them looked at Alan's tent. His death felt like a specter none of them wanted to acknowledge if they could help it. Tulia couldn't blame John and Carolyn for wanting to leave. This was near the top of her list as one of the worst camping trips she had ever had.

CHAPTER NINE

Once the preparations for the storm were complete, everyone split up to spend some time on their own. The strain and tension was getting to the group. John and Carolyn took a walk out to the river, while Robert disappeared into his tent and Loren dragged a camp chair over to Alan's tent and sat outside it, his jaw clenched.

Samuel and Tulia walked back up the hill and sat at the top of it, taking in the view and occasionally chatting about the case. He made the call to Amelia when he was ready, and Tulia had to dab tears away from her eyes as she listened to his half of the conversation. He was careful to only tell her the fact of what they had learned, nothing about their suspicions and guesses. She hoped they would have something more solid to tell her when they got back to Loon Bay.

They didn't have much to go on, and Tulia didn't know if the uneasiness that hung over the camp was due to the circumstances of Alan's death, or just the fact of it. She was tired, she felt grungy and gross since she hadn't been able to shower since the morning before they left, and her back was still sore from the night on the ground.

She didn't regret coming here with Samuel, but it was a good reminder that most of his job wasn't glamorous. There was a big difference between the traveling for work he did, and the traveling for fun she had done. Not that she hadn't gotten embroiled in her own share of adventures, but she had always known that she could just leave the area if it all got to be too much for her. Other than common human kindness, she hadn't had a responsibility to help any of the people she had met. Somehow, the knowledge that they were here on a *job* made everything seem to weigh much heavier on her shoulders.

"Do you think Marc and Violet are worried?" she asked when he ended the call with Amelia. "Should we call them?"

"I'll leave a message on the office machine," he

said. "Remember, there's a time difference. I don't want to wake them up. I thought updating Amelia was important enough to disturb her, but we don't have anything urgent to share with Marc and Violet yet."

"I hope Cicero is doing all right. I feel bad leaving so suddenly while he's still getting used to the new apartment."

"He likes Violet," Samuel assured her. "He'll be all right. He's a good bird."

"Yeah, he is." She smiled a little and leaned against him. He put his arm around her waist, holding her closer.

"I know you haven't had much time to settle in, but how do you like Loon Bay so far?"

"I love it. I love the view from my apartment, and the fact that I can walk almost everywhere, and the small town feel even though it's so close to Boston. I love living right by the ocean. And I love being more involved with the private investigative agency."

"That's all?" he asked, sounding amused.

She grinned. "Well, I suppose I love being closer to you too. Not that it was my main reason for moving out there or anything."

"Of course," he said with a chuckle.

Sometimes she was still astonished at how her life

had turned out. She had been a waitress sharing an apartment with her boyfriend not even two years ago, and her life hadn't been … bad, exactly. It had been perfectly average. She had always wanted something more, but she hadn't known enough to know what that *more* was.

Sometimes, she wondered if she ever would have made the changes she needed to make if she hadn't won the lottery. She didn't like thinking that the person she was now had only come into being because of the ridiculous sum of money she had lucked into. But while the money had made her journey a lot easier, and let her travel in style, and move to another state without much worry about what would happen if it didn't work out, she hadn't done anything that would be *impossible* without it. She could have taken a trip around the country even before she had the lottery winnings. She could have gotten a remote job, bought an old SUV or a cheap camper trailer, and made it work. She liked to think that eventually she would have gotten her head on straight and done just that, but she supposed she would never know.

They sat up there on the hill until the sun started going down and the smell of cooking fish drifted over to them. After only one meal of the fresh fish, Tulia was already starting to wish for something else. It wasn't *bad*, but the only thing they had to season it with was some salt. But she wasn't about to complain when she knew they were limited on food supplies. Carolyn had her own stash of food, since she was a vegetarian who didn't eat fish, though she had accepted a few granola bars in exchange for some dried cranberries earlier.

"Let's head back," she said, standing up with a sigh and brushing off her jeans before reaching her hand down to Samuel.

"We might not have to wait the whole forty-eight hours," Samuel reminded her as they started the trek back down the hill. "That was the longest timeframe they gave me. If the storm changes course, they might come earlier."

"We'll have to hope for that," she said. She didn't know if it was her imagination, but she thought there was a strange charge in the air, like the threat of approaching rain. The sky was hazy off in the distance, but the storm clouds had yet to truly appear.

They ate a mostly silent dinner with the others, then John and Carolyn went off to the river to clean the dishes by themselves. Everyone else returned to their tents, so Tulia and Samuel did the same. The days were long this far north, but she had done a lot more physical work than she was used to, and she was tired despite the fact that the sun was still out. There wasn't much else to do except for sleep, so they went to bed early that night.

Perhaps that was why she woke up a few hours later, after the sun had dipped behind the mountains. Samuel was snoring quietly on his sleeping roll, and she could hear the drone of insects around them. The air felt cooler than it had earlier, and she thought she could hear a rumble of thunder in the distance.

But that wasn't what had woken her up. It was the sound of a zipper closing. Someone else was up. Tulia got to her knees and slowly unzipped the flap that covered the screen at the front of the tent. She peeked outside to see that someone was sitting in one of the camp chairs by the glowing embers of the fire. Judging by the person's long hair, it was Carolyn. It looked like she was packing something into her back-pack. Tulia frowned. Was the woman planning on going somewhere this late?

She remembered what Robert had said about how dangerous the storm could be, and Carolyn's dissatis-faction at having to stay any longer. Deciding that she had to at least say something if the woman was plan-ning on trying to hike back to the SUV by herself, she unzipped the tent door and stepped outside. Carolyn looked around when she saw her but didn't say anything until Tulia took the seat next to her.

"Sorry if I woke you," she whispered.

"It's okay," Tulia whispered back. "If it wasn't you, it would have been the thunder or the rock that was digging into my back."

Carolyn gave a small smile and finished zipping the side pocket of her backpack up. "I used to love coming out here," she said quietly. "Before I met John, I was never one for hiking or enjoying the great outdoors, but he taught me how to love it. I don't know if I'll ever be able to enjoy it like I used to after this. I hope John will retire at last, stop doing tours. It's not so bad when it's just friends, but I hate it when he goes off with strangers for days or even weeks at a time. This isn't the first time he's gotten hurt, and I know there's always a chance he might not come back."

"He seems to know what he's doing," Tulia said.

"Oh, he does. But sometimes accidents just … happen, and there's nothing you can do to stop them. When everyone else got sick that night, I was so worried I was about to lose my husband. Alan's death was bad enough, but I can't stop thinking about what would have happened if John had died too. All because of one simple mistake."

"The food poisoning?"

Carolyn nodded. "We must have left the meat out for too long or not cooked it right... I just don't know, but it drove home how easily things can go wrong out here, and when they do, there's no help."

"Is that why it looks like you're about to head off into the night by yourself?"

Carolyn looked down at her backpack and snorted. "Oh, I guess that *is* what it looks like. No, I'm just making sure I have everything ready for the morning. I saw lightning flashes off in the distance. I'm hopeful that means the storm is passing by a few miles away from us. If it does, we can all start heading back. I know the others don't want to leave Alan's body here, but the sooner we get out of here, the better. I feel like I'm going crazy out here."

Tulia felt like she was going crazy after just two days here. She couldn't even imagine what the others were going through, knowing their friend was dead in a tent just feet away from where they were sleeping and not being able to do anything about it. She squeezed the woman's hand briefly before standing back up.

"It'll all be over soon," she said. "I don't think you're the only one who wants to get out of here. As long as that storm passes us by, I'm guessing we'll head out as a group."

Carolyn gave her a grateful smile, and Tulia returned to her tent, leaving the other woman staring into the embers alone.

CHAPTER TEN

Tulia managed to get back to sleep without too much trouble, mostly because there was nothing else she could do. Not having any phone service prevented her from scrolling mindlessly on social media, or even checking her blog. She spent the time before she slept mentally writing her next blog post. She wouldn't mention anything about the case, but she would certainly mention Alaska's gorgeous scenery and the sheer, wild feel of it.

She woke up sore and feeling even more disgusting than she had the previous morning. She brushed her teeth, wished she had thought to bring some dry shampoo, and changed into her last set of clean clothing. The feeling of being unwashed made her grumpy. She thought about trying to bathe in the river, but she had felt how cold the water was when she helped get more water for the group the day before and wasn't sure if she could bear it.

Loren was the first one up that morning, but he had ignored her while she went through her modified morning routine. By the time Samuel joined her, Robert was also up. Then Carolyn came out of her tent, looking almost eager as she glanced at the sky.

"It's definitely cloudy over to the southeast, but it looks like the storm passed us by last night. The clouds are moving away from us. What do you think, should we try to make it back to the vehicles?"

She looked around, then frowned. "Where's John?"

"I haven't seen him," Loren said. "I thought I was the first one up."

"Well, he's not in the tent. And he was there when I went back to sleep last night. No one has seen him this morning?"

They all shook their heads. A surge of energy went through the group as they realized one of their members was missing.

Carolyn ducked back into the tent to try to figure out what had happened. Robert announced he was going down to the fishing spot at the river to see if John had gone there, but before he left, Carolyn came back out of the tent, holding a piece of paper torn out of a legal pad.

"He left," she said, her voice tight with worry. "He put a note on his sleeping bag. I didn't notice it when I got up. It says he woke up early and he saw that the storm passed us, and he's going to go back to the SUV and find someone who can get some all-terrain vehicles out here to help us."

"Is this like him?" Samuel asked. "Does he normally go off and do things on his own like this?"

Carolyn glared at the paper. "No! Well, he's always been independent, and always thinks he knows what's best when we're out hiking, but I can't believe he left me behind. He knew how much I wanted to get back."

"Should we go look for him?" Robert asked.

"How long have you been up, Loren?" Tulia asked.

He frowned. "Maybe two hours? I woke up pretty early. And no, I didn't see him at all. He's been gone for at least that long."

"Then there's probably no way we can catch him," Robert muttered. "Should the rest of us pack up and start walking back too? That's what we were planning on doing, right?"

"We can't leave Alan's body," Loren said. "At least one person should stay with it."

"Since the storm passed this area by, the rescue team should come for us today," Samuel said. "We also have John going for help. He will reach the road long before we would. Between him and the rescue team, I think it's best that we just wait here. If we're here, they'll know where to find us, but if we try to head back ourselves, we might pass John or the rescue team and not realize it."

"I can't wait here any longer," Carolyn said. "I don't understand why he wouldn't *wait* for me."

"Because John never takes anyone else's opinions into consideration," Robert snapped back. "He likes being the big head-honcho of our group, and he didn't like everyone convincing him to stay last night. I bet he did this just to prove he knows what's best."

"You can't talk about John like that," Carolyn said. "He practically raised you and Alan."

"He didn't raise us, he paid us two dollars an hour to help out on his tours when we were teens. That's all."

Carolyn gaped, offense flashing across her face. Before she could say anything else, Samuel stepped forward, raising his hands.

"I think we all need to take a deep breath and give

each other some space," he said. "We are almost guaranteed to get out of here today, either with John's help or the authorities' help. Why don't we all take some time to cool off?"

An angry silence followed his words, but one by one, the others stomped away, back into their tents. Tulia and Samuel retreated to their own safe haven, sitting inside the tent with the door open so they could see if the others approached.

"I don't like this," Samuel muttered. "Things are devolving here. I hope the rescue team really does come today."

"I don't blame Carolyn for being mad," Tulia muttered, staring at the woman's tent. "Her husband left her behind without saying a word. I'd be pretty mad too."

"Mad or not, we all need to work together. Just because that storm didn't hit us, it doesn't mean everything is hunky-dory. I know Alan's death is wearing on them, but if someone throws a punch and someone else gets hurt, we're out of luck. There aren't any hospitals around here."

"I hate this," Tulia said with a sigh. "I feel so useless. We can't *do* anything. We have to sit here and babysit this group of adults to make sure they don't kill each other."

"No, we don't," Samuel said. He rose to his feet and helped her up. "They're all hidden away in their tents for now anyway, and you're right. They are adults. We don't have to babysit them. Let's take a walk. We'll both feel better once we blow off some steam."

She agreed with that. They decided to walk back down to the fishing spot, where they had cleaned off the pans the day before. It was a few minutes away, but as soon as they were out of sight of the camp, she felt some of the tension leave her shoulders. For a little while, she could pretend they were on a lovely vacation and nothing more.

When they reached the river, she took off her socks and shoes and dipped her feet into it. It was frigid, but it still felt good. There were footsteps in the muddy sand at the bank of the river, showing how often the others had come here to fish.

"They must come here a lot," she mused. "It seems like it's a favorite spot for them."

"I doubt they will be able to come here again without thinking about what happened to Alan," Samuel said. "Food poisoning." He sighed. "The kicker is, I still don't know if I believe it or not."

Tulia heaved her own sigh and walked barefoot down the bank a little way. There was something like a game trail leading away from the river, so she followed it, gazing out at the scenery. She definitely wanted to come back at some point. Maybe not to this exact spot, but back to Alaska in general. Maybe she could convince her parents to come with her and they could take a guided backpacking trip … with someone other than John Grant leading them.

She was about to turn back and rejoin Samuel at the fishing spot when she noticed a dug-up patch of earth. The unnatural glint of foil in the sunlight caught her attention. Frowning, she walked over to see what it was, then jumped back when she saw a large animal print.

"Samuel!" she called out. He hurried to where she was and looked at where she was pointing, then let out a low whistle.

"That's from a bear."

"It looks fresh, doesn't it?"

"It must've come during the night. What was it digging up?"

"It looks like food wrappers," she said. She recognized some meat packaging, and what looked like a torn open package of cheese.

"Why would someone bury a bunch of food here?" he asked. "Hold on, didn't they say they disposed of the food they thought might have caused the food poisoning?"

She frowned. She did remember that, sort of.

"Look," she said, stooping down to pick something up out of the dirt. "What are these berries? That's weird. I thought they were yogurt drops at first. I've never seen white berries before."

"Huh," Samuel said, taking the bag from her and holding it up to the sunlight. "That's weird. It's the only thing the bear didn't eat."

"Look at the label on the bag. It says it's supposed to be cheese, but that is definitely not cheese."

His frown deepened as he looked at the berries. "Let's head back. I want to check that survival guide we got. I don't know much about berries or foraging, but I'm pretty sure white berries aren't usually safe to eat. I want to see if we can identify them with that book."

She nodded and followed him back down to the fishing spot, where she put on her shoes. She kept her head on a swivel just in case the bear had lingered in the area, but thankfully, she didn't see it.

Dealing with some grumpy fellow campers was one thing. A hungry bear was another thing entirely.

CHAPTER ELEVEN

They never even made it back to their tent. Almost as soon as they stepped into camp, Robert and Loren zeroed in on them.

"We were talking, and we decided—" He broke off, staring at the bag of berries in Samuel's hand. "What is that? Where did you get those?"

"You know what they are?" Samuel asked.

"Those are baneberries," Robert said. "They're deadly. You haven't eaten any, have you?"

"No, we found them," Tulia said. She looked at the bag with new concern. No wonder the bear hadn't eaten them. She wasn't stupid enough to think tasting them a good idea, but she was glad they had found them before some other backpacking group made their way through the area. If a child found them, or someone hungry enough to risk it...

"Good," Robert said. "You shouldn't have even picked them. Just a few of them is enough to kill a grown man."

"They were already in the bag when we found them," Samuel said slowly. "It looks like they were buried by the river, but a bear dug them up."

"A bear?" Loren spoke up, his eyes wide. "There's a *bear* near the campsite?"

"It must've smelled that food we buried earlier," Robert mused. "We should have buried it further away. We were all too sick to do more than the bare minimum, though. Carolyn's the one we sent out to do it. I'm not surprised she stayed so close to camp, that was a bad day."

"What were poisonous berries doing with our food?" Loren asked. "Forget food poisoning. Alan must've eaten some of *these*."

Tulia exchanged a wide-eyed look with Samuel. That explanation certainly made a lot more sense than random, fatal food poisoning.

"You and John were the ones who cooked," Robert snapped at him. "Did you add some of these to the meal?"

"No way," Loren said. "All I did was cut up some

AXED IN ALASKA   85

meat. John's the one who was in charge of most of the ingredients."

"The berries must've gotten into the food *somehow*," Robert said. "And that doesn't explain how they got into that bag in the first place. None of us would have picked the berries. We all know better."

"Hold on," Tulia said. "Where's Carolyn?"

Robert shrugged. "She said she was taking a walk. I don't know where she went."

"Maybe John picked the berries for some reason," Loren said. "He always seems to be gathering and collecting random things."

"John would never throw *poisonous berries* into our meal," Robert said. "Unless you're saying he tried to kill all of us."

"You forgot that Alan was helping with the food too," Loren said hesitantly. "I hate to say it, but maybe he did it?"

"You're saying that my dead best friend might have tried to *murder* us all, and then somehow forgot he added the berries and ate the very food he poisoned?" Robert sounded disgusted.

"No! I meant accidentally. Maybe he just … didn't recognize them."

"Alan grew up here," Robert said. "Of course he

would recognize baneberries."

"Then if it wasn't him, maybe Carolyn," Loren said. "She's the only one who didn't eat any of the meat."

"Yeah, because she's a vegetarian," Robert said testily.

This was not going well.

"We should try to find Carolyn," Tulia chimed in. "If we're going to talk about this, we should all be here. She might have seen something no one else did."

"Well, I don't know where she went," Robert said. "She just said she was going on a walk."

"Did she have her backpack with her?" Samuel asked.

Robert frowned. "I don't remember."

Tulia felt her stomach clench. Of course. Carolyn had been so eager to get back to the car. And so mad that John had left her behind. She must have gone after him.

"One of us should check their tent to see if she took it," Samuel said.

"I'll do it," Tulia said. She figured that the people doing the investigating should be her and Samuel, since that was their *job*, and she didn't want to be left alone to play referee with these two arguing men.

Leaving Samuel holding the berries, she hurried away and unzipped Carolyn and John's tent. Both of their sleeping bags were still inside it, and to her relief, she saw Carolyn's backpack tucked into the corner.

So Carolyn hadn't gone back to the SUV after all. That was good news. She glanced back toward the others, but they were still embroiled in their argument, so she slipped into the tent and sat next to the backpack, looking at it. She was curious as to what Carolyn had been doing with it the night before. It didn't make any sense that she would be out by the fire packing when all of her belongings were in this tent.

Carefully, she unzipped the backpack and started going through it, being careful not to disturb the contents too much. She didn't find anything interesting, though there was a bottle of dry shampoo she was very envious of, until, tucked securely into the zipped side pocket, she found a checkbook. It struck her as such a random thing to have out here in the middle of nowhere. Who paid with checks these days, anyway? She picked it up and flipped through idly until she realized the name that was on the checks wasn't Carolyn's.

This checkbook belonged to Alan Casey.

Frowning, she took a more careful look at what

was inside. There were only a few used checks, which he seemed to have used to pay his rent. But the very last one, which hadn't been torn out yet, was addressed to Carolyn.

The sum on it made her gasp. It was for two million dollars, and on the line that said what the payment was for was written only the word *Gift*. The check was signed, but she couldn't stop staring at it, because she had never seen such a big number on a check before. Sure, she was used to the numbers in her bank account, but it seemed much more real somehow, looking at it on paper.

For some reason, Alan had been about to pay Carolyn two million dollars. The check was dated for the night of the food poisoning incident.

A woman's voice alerted her that Carolyn was returning. She slipped the checkbook into her pocket, zipped the bag back up, and stepped out of the tent in time to see the other woman stomping across the campground.

"Why is everyone arguing again?" Carolyn snapped. "What's going on? Can't I have a moment of—" She broke off, inhaling sharply.

Her eyes were fixed on the bag of white berries Samuel was holding.

CHAPTER TWELVE

"Where did you get those?" Carolyn asked. She looked pale and didn't even seem to notice that Tulia had come out of her tent.

"We found them," Samuel said.

"I already told him they're poisonous," Robert said. "They didn't eat any, but we're trying to figure out why they were buried with all of the food we got rid of."

Samuel was staring at Carolyn, his brows furrowed. Tulia wished she had the chance to tell him about the checkbook she had found, but there was no way to get him away from the others right now.

"How … how did you find the food?" Carolyn asked.

"A bear dug it up," Loren said. "A freaking bear.

Super close to our camp. Right next to the fishing spot. *This* is why I'm glad I live in Boston, where wild animals don't walk around looking to eat you."

"We're worried the berries might be the reason for Alan's death, not just regular food poisoning," Samuel told her.

Carolyn took a step back. "You think someone murdered Alan?"

"If that's true, then whoever it was almost murdered all of us," Robert said. "We all got sick. All of us except for you."

"This is too much for me," Carolyn said faintly. "We should go back. Now. I can't handle this anymore."

She stumbled away from them, then turned and hurried past Tulia and into her tent.

"I agree," Robert said. "Forget waiting for rescue. Let's get out of here."

"What about Alan?" Loren said. "Did you forget there's a *bear* out here? What if it finds him?"

"I'd rather the bear find someone who's already dead than have it find whoever waits here," Robert snapped.

Behind her, in the tent, Tulia heard the increasingly frantic sounds of Carolyn throwing things around.

"Did one of you go through my things?" Carolyn asked, poking her head out of the tent. "I'm missing something important."

"The only one in there was Tulia," Robert said as he turned to walk toward his own tent. "And she was only in there to see if you took your backpack with you. We thought you might have left to go after John."

Tulia started walking back toward Samuel, who was looking at her in concern. Carolyn's eyes snapped toward her. Hesitantly, Tulia took the checkbook out of her pocket.

"Are you looking for this?"

Carolyn's eyes widened.

"What is that?" Samuel asked.

"It's a checkbook," Tulia said slowly. "Alan's checkbook. He wrote Carolyn a check for two million dollars the day he died."

That got everyone's attention. Robert froze, and Loren came back out of his tent, his eyes narrowing.

"No, he didn't."

"I have proof right here," Tulia said.

"Alan wasn't going to give anyone money," Loren said. "Not yet. He was going to talk to his lawyers first and figure out a plan. He did not write her a check."

"Why would he write Carolyn a check when he wouldn't even give *me* any money?" Robert asked, his voice dangerous. "I begged him, not even for *half* like he promised, but for a few hundred thousand dollars. I was his best friend for *years*. There's no way he would have written her a check instead of me."

Now both men were looking at Carolyn dangerously. She climbed out of her tent and stood with her hands on her hips, though she looked a little uncertain. "It's no business of yours if he agreed to help my husband and me out in our time of need."

"Why does the checkbook matter now?" Samuel asked. They all looked over at him. Tulia continued backing up until she was by his side. She held onto the checkbook tightly, worried Carolyn was going to rush at her and try to take it away.

"I'm not sure what you mean," Carolyn said.

"He's dead. Whatever's going to happen with his estate, I doubt that check will be honored. Especially for that amount."

"Are you sure he wrote it himself?" Loren asked. "I was with him when he won. He didn't even tell his fiancée about this. I'm telling you, he wouldn't have given money like that to anyone."

The question about whether he wrote the check

himself made Tulia flip the checkbook open again. She scrutinized the signature on the check for two million dollars, then flipped up to one of the carbon copies of a rent check. She frowned. The signatures looked similar, but not quite the same. All of the other signatures on the carbon copies were almost identical, but there was something off about the last one.

"This doesn't really look like his signature," she said at last.

"Well, it is," Carolyn snapped. "He signed that check, and it's real. You're stealing a fortune from me if you keep it, and I *will* press charges." She stomped forward and held her hand out, but Tulia kept her grip on the checkbook.

"You would have known about the baneberries," Robert said slowly. "Anyone who spends any time out here knows to avoid them. And ... you didn't eat any of the food we made. But if I remember correctly, you helped to serve it."

"That's right, she did," Loren said. "She handed everyone their plates."

"What are you saying?" Carolyn said. "You think I poisoned everyone after Alan agreed to give me some of his winnings? I would have to be insane to do that."

"Maybe you didn't try to poison everyone, just

him," Loren said. "I saw you almost drop his plate when you were spooning food onto it. You could have dropped some of the berries into the pot then too, without realizing it."

Carolyn looked back and forth between them, her eyes wide. "This … this is absurd."

"Why were you so eager to get back to civilization?" Tulia asked. "When I talked to you last night, you said you were going to set off this morning. The rescue team is going to come today, so waiting would be smarter. You were always the one pushing to leave, you even tried to get John to go with you yesterday afternoon."

"I just didn't feel like being out here anymore," Carolyn said, her voice climbing in pitch. "Why is that so unbelievable?"

"You were very insistent about you and John going back first, while the rest of us waited here," Robert said. "I bet you were going to try to cash that check before the authorities knew Alan was dead."

Carolyn looked like she was about to have a panic attack. Tulia would have felt bad for her, but she was *certain* they were on the right track.

"Loren told me everyone was asking Alan for money," she said quietly. "That means you must have asked too. And he said no, didn't he? But you didn't take that for an answer. You killed him and then you forged that check and planned to cash it before anyone realized what had happened."

Carolyn didn't respond. She wiped her eyes, looking very upset and very alone. All of a sudden, one more thing made sense to Tulia.

"Did John find the checkbook? Is that why he left so early?"

Carolyn's eyes widened in realization. "He saw it," she breathed. "He knew. Oh, my goodness, he's never going to forgive me. He saw Alan as *family*. He was never supposed to find out. That money was to give us the retirement we deserve!"

She lunged toward Tulia and the checkbook, but Tulia darted behind Samuel, who grabbed Carolyn's wrists to keep her away from them. Robert and Loren pulled her back.

"It's not fair," Carolyn wailed. "He should have agreed to help us! We deserved one good thing, after all we did for him. I don't understand why he wouldn't give me something."

"He was going to," Loren snarled. "He was going to give all of his friends something from his winnings. He just wanted to get all of his ducks in a row first. But you killed him on what should have been the best vacation of his life, and he's never going to get to do all of the things he dreamed of."

Carolyn broke down into tears. The rest of them fell silent. In the quiet, Tulia noticed a new sound, a strange thudding she could feel in her bones.

"What is that?"

Samuel turned and started scanning the skies. "It sounds like a helicopter," he said. "I think our rescue is here."

EPILOGUE

She was a little surprised when stepping into her apartment after getting back from Alaska felt like stepping into her *home*. Cicero whistled at her from his cage, and as soon as she got her shoes off and deposited her bags on the couch, she hurried over to take him out of the cage and kiss his beak.

"I'm sorry I was gone for so long, buddy," she said. "I missed you. Did you have a nice time with Violet?"

She knew he had. Violet and Marc had picked her and Samuel up from the airport, and on the ride back to Loon Bay, Violet had told her all about her time with Cicero. The bird had been on his best behavior, though Violet was worried he might have picked up some of her concern for Tulia and Samuel when they went off grid.

It had been an intense trip, and while Tulia was glad she had gone with Samuel, she was also glad to be back. Her life in Loon Bay was just getting started. She wasn't about to stop traveling, but she wanted to settle into her new home before she went anywhere else.

Samuel, on the other hand, seemed to have been bitten by the travel bug. During the long flight back to Massachusetts, they had made plans for their next trip. It would be pure fun this time, no work, and no investigations.

Tulia was excited. They weren't leaving for a couple of months, but when they did go, it was to a brand-new destination. Somewhere she had been wanting to go for a long time. She was going to need an updated passport, and she had to do a lot of research, but all of the effort it took to plan the trip would be worth it.

This fall, she and Samuel were going to Europe, just the two of them. It was high time they took a vacation together, one that didn't have any purpose besides enjoying themselves and relaxing.

A *real* vacation. She could hardly wait.

Made in the USA
Coppell, TX
15 November 2023

24291662R00069